My Secret Unicorn

A Touch of Magic

Lauren didn't sleep well that night. She couldn't stop worrying about Max. He had looked after Buddy for the rest of the day, feeding him and brushing him, but he had done it sulkily and Lauren had noticed their mom frowning as she watched him. *If only Buddy could talk to him like Twilight can talk to me,* Lauren thought as she turned over restlessly in bed. *Then he'd be able to tell Max how he feels.*

My Secret Unicorn

A Touch of Magic

Linda Chapman

Illustrated by Ann Kronheimer

Cover Illustration by Andrew Farley

SCHOLASTIC INC.

New York   Toronto   London   Auckland   Sydney
Mexico City   New Delhi   Hong Kong   Buenos Aires

ISBN 0-439-79595-8

12   11   10   9   8   7   6   5   4   6   7   8   9   10/0

Printed in the U.S.A.   40
First Scholastic printing, December 2005

To Holly and Charlotte Allison

My Secret Unicorn

Unicorn

A Touch of Magic

CHAPTER

One

Three strides, two strides, one stride . . .
Twilight soared through the
air and landed safely on the other side of
the jump.

"Good boy!" Lauren Foster exclaimed,
patting his neck. Mel and Jessica, Lauren's
two best friends, clapped from where they
were sitting on their ponies, Shadow and
Sandy. The three girls had spent an hour

after school putting up a course of jumps in the field at Mel's farm.

"It's like he's flying!" Mel called.

Lauren bit back a grin. If only Mel knew her secret! Even though Twilight looked like an ordinary pony most of the time, when Lauren said the magic words, he turned into a snowy-white unicorn who actually *could* fly. The only people who knew the truth were an older woman named Mrs. Fontana and Lauren's friend Michael, who lived in the city and had a secret unicorn pony of his own.

Lauren pointed Twilight toward the final fence. Mel had decided to put a row of flowerpots in front, which made it look enormous.

Lauren gulped. Suddenly, she wasn't so sure about jumping it. *What if Twilight fell . . . ?*

Twilight slowed down.

Lauren clicked her tongue, but Twilight got slower still. He was going to refuse! Lauren forced down her fear. "Come on, Twilight!" she cried, pressing him on. Twilight sped up again and they flew over it.

"Good boy!" Lauren sighed with relief as they landed safely.

"That was great," Mel said as Lauren trotted over.

"I didn't think I was going to make the last fence," Lauren replied. "Twilight slowed down a lot."

Mel frowned. "That's not like Twilight. He hasn't hurt himself, has he?"

Lauren felt a flicker of alarm. "I don't know." Dismounting, she checked Twilight's legs. There were no obvious cuts or scrapes. She picked up his hooves, but they were clear of stones. "He seems all right."

"Maybe it was just the jump that made him slow down," Jessica suggested. "It *is* really big."

"Yeah," Lauren agreed. "Those flower-pots make it look huge." She noticed that the sun had started to set beyond the mountains that rose up in the distance. "I'd better go. Are we going to meet up tomorrow and do our school project?"

"Definitely," said Mel. "We've still got lots to do. We've got to make our project the best!"

For the last few days, their class at school had been working in groups.

They'd had to choose a hobby to talk about and the following week they were going to make presentations to the class. Lauren, Mel, and Jessica had naturally decided to do their project on ponies.

"I wish Jade's and David's groups weren't riding horses, also." Jessica sighed.

Mel nodded. "The people who aren't into ponies are going to get really bored listening to three talks about the same thing."

"We'll just have to think of some way to make our project different," Lauren said. "We can do that tomorrow." She squeezed Twilight on. "See you guys in the morning."

As Lauren rode Twilight up the drive-way that linked Mel's farm with the road, the last few rays of the sun glowed on Twilight's mane. "You were great today," Lauren told him. Then she remembered how he had slowed down at the last jump. "You are OK, though, aren't you? You're not hurt?"

Twilight snorted.

Lauren wondered what a snort meant. She knew Twilight understood every word she said, but he could only talk back to her when he was a unicorn. She felt slightly alarmed. Maybe there *was* something wrong and he was trying to tell her!

They reached the end of the drive. Lauren normally turned right toward Granger's Farm, where she lived with her mom, dad, and younger brother, Max. But now she hesitated. There was a wooded area on the other side of the road. If she rode into the trees, she could turn Twilight into a unicorn and ask him if there was anything wrong.

She checked the road. It was empty. "Come on, Twilight," she whispered. "I'm going to turn you into a unicorn."

They entered the trees. Once they were hidden from sight, Lauren jumped off

Twilight's back and said the magic words
of the Turning Spell:

> *"Twilight Star, Twilight Star,*
> *Twinkling high above so far.*
> *Shining light, shining bright,*
> *Will you grant my wish tonight?*
> *Let my little horse forlorn*
> *Be at last a unicorn!"*

There was a bright purple flash and,
suddenly, Twilight was no longer a scruffy
gray pony. Instead he had transformed into
a beautiful unicorn with a snowy coat and
a gleaming silver horn in the center of his
forehead.

"Twilight!" Lauren exclaimed, hugging him.

Twilight tossed his silvery mane. "Hi, Lauren." His mouth didn't move but as long as Lauren was either touching him or holding a hair from his mane, she could hear him speaking as clearly as if he were another human being.

"Are you OK?" Lauren asked anx-
iously. "Why did you slow down at that
last fence?"

"It felt like you didn't really want to
jump it," Twilight replied. "As we were
going toward it, you pulled on the reins
and stopped pressing me on. I didn't want
to jump if you were frightened."

Lauren remembered the way her stomach had somersaulted when she had turned
in toward the fence. "I guess I was scared
for a few seconds," she admitted. "I'm
sorry I pulled on your mouth."

"That's OK," Twilight replied, rubbing
his ears against her while being careful not
to catch her with his horn. "You didn't
pull hard."

Lauren gave him a hug. She was very relieved to find out that he wasn't hurt. "I'd better turn you back now," she told him. "Mom and Dad will be wondering where I am. But I'll come to your field later and we can go flying."

She said the words of the Undoing Spell and Twilight turned back into a pony.

Lauren mounted and rode out of the trees. As Twilight's hooves clip-clopped along the quiet road, she thought how lucky she was to be able to talk to him. It meant she could always find out if there was anything wrong. She felt her heart swell with love. She had a secret unicorn of her own! Oh, yes, she was very lucky indeed.

CHAPTER

Two

"You've been riding late," said her
dad as Lauren walked into the
kitchen a little while later.

"Mel, Jessica, and I were jumping,"
Lauren explained, sitting down to pull off
her boots. Buddy, Max's dog, trotted over
to say hello. He was a young Bernese
mountain dog and almost as big as a small
Shetland pony. He plonked his heavy head

in her lap and Lauren patted him. "Where's Mom?" she asked.

"Working in her study," her dad replied. "I said I'd fix supper tonight."

Lauren's mom was a writer and she often shut herself in her study for hours at a time when she was trying to finish a book.

Mr. Foster stirred some pasta into a pot of boiling water on the stove. "So, it's Saturday tomorrow. What're you up to? Are you seeing Mel and Jessica?"

"Yes," Lauren replied, scratching Buddy's ears. "We're doing a project together on our favorite hobby. We've got to give a talk in front of the whole class." She frowned. "I just hope it's interesting enough, Dad. Two other groups are doing their projects on horses, too."

"I'm sure you'll think of something to make your project stand out," Mr. Foster said comfortingly.

"I hope so." Lauren sighed.

Buddy wriggled around so he was sitting on her feet. He pressed against Lauren's legs, his tail thumping. Lauren laughed. "Buddy's being extra affectionate tonight."

"I don't think Max has fed him yet." Mr. Foster went to the kitchen door. "Max, come and feed Buddy, please!"

"In a minute!" Lauren heard her seven-year-old brother call back from the living room.

"Now," Mr. Foster insisted.

"What's Max doing?" Lauren asked.

"Watching some DVD about skate-boarding," Mr. Foster replied. "Steven and Leo lent it to him."

Lauren nodded. Ever since Steven and Leo Vance had moved into a house just down the road, Max had been really into skateboarding. Leo and Steven, who were eight and ten years old, both had skate-boards, and Max had been playing with them on the weekends and after school.

Max came into the kitchen looking grumpy. "It was just at a really good part, Dad."

Mr. Foster shrugged. "Sorry, Max, but

Buddy needs feeding. DVDs can wait.
Animals can't."

Max sighed but fetched Buddy's bowl.
With his curly brown hair and brown eyes,
he looked just like a smaller version of
their dad.

"Is it a good DVD?" Lauren asked him.

Max's eyes lit up. "It's great! It shows

you how to do all these jumps. Leo and Steven can do lots of them and I'm going to learn, too. I did a real Ollie today!"

"Oh . . . that's good," Lauren said, not having a clue what an Ollie was.

"I'm going over to their house tomorrow to practice some more." Max put Buddy's bowl of food down.

"Maybe you should invite Leo and Steven over here, Max," Mr. Foster suggested. "You always seem to be going to their house."

"That's because they've got a great place to skate," Max replied. "They've got a launch ramp *and* a quarter pipe to practice on."

"Well, we could make something here," Mr. Foster said. "You could use that concrete area near Twilight's field — the place where the old barn was. I could construct a ramp or two."

Max looked at him in delight. "Really?"

Mr. Foster nodded. "I'll see what I can do. However, I don't want to see you forgetting Buddy's supper again, Max. Having a pet is a big responsibility. You have to think of his needs before your own."

"I'll feed Buddy on time from now on, I promise," Max said happily. He stroked Buddy. "Sorry, boy." Buddy looked up from licking his bowl clean and wagged his tail.

Mr. Foster smiled. "OK, you can go watch some more of your DVD. But only ten minutes and then it's suppertime."

Max ran out of the room. Lauren watched him go. She couldn't understand his new craze for skateboarding. It seemed to be all he was interested in at the moment.

Buddy came over and she petted him.

Her dad was right. Since Max had started skateboarding, he hadn't been spending nearly as much time with Buddy as he used to. Lauren could feel tangles in the thick white fur around Buddy's collar. When had Max last brushed him? She wasn't sure. Bending down, she kissed the overgrown puppy. She hoped Max was going to start giving him some more attention soon.

That night, when her parents had gone to bed, Lauren crept out to Twilight's field. He was waiting by the gate.

Lauren wasted no time. She whispered the words of the Turning Spell and Twilight became a unicorn once again.

"Sorry I'm late," Lauren said. "Mom and Dad stayed up later than usual." She scrambled onto Twilight's warm back. "Let's go flying!"

Twilight whinnied in delight and plunged into the sky. They flew up and up. Lauren's long blond hair blew back from her face but she felt wrapped in warmth. Twilight's magic meant she never felt cold when they were flying — and she never felt tired afterward. Twilight could do all kinds of magic — special magic to help other people or animals in danger. He could heal wounds, make people feel brave, cut a path through snow, and see things that were happening far away. He had other powers, too — powers that he and Lauren were still finding out about.

Suddenly, Twilight slowed down. "Listen, Lauren! Can you hear that noise? It sounds like an animal in trouble."

Listening hard, Lauren heard it, too. A panicked squeaking noise was coming from the ground beneath them. "Quick!" she said. "Let's go see what it is!"

CHAPTER

Three

Twilight landed in a clearing.

"The noise is coming from over there," he said, pointing with his horn to a tangle of prickly hawthorn at the edge of the clearing.

Jumping off Twilight's back, Lauren went to investigate. "Look, Twilight!"

It was very dark but Lauren could see that a baby squirrel was caught in the

depths of the thicket. Its thick bushy
tail was tangled up in thorns, and it was
struggling desperately.

"Poor little thing!" Lauren exclaimed.
She flung herself down on her stomach
and pushed her arm through the thorny
branches. The squirrel's black eyes darted
around frantically.

"It's OK. I'm here to help you,"
Lauren soothed. "Ow!" she cried as the
thorns raked down her arm.

"Here, let me help," Twilight offered.
He bent down and started to push the
bushes aside with his horn.

There was a vivid purple flash and a
cloud of smoke. Lauren gasped and
Twilight snorted in surprise. Even the

squirrel stopped squeaking for a moment and stared.

The long branches had started to unwind from one another as if they had come alive.

"The brambles, Twilight!" cried Lauren. "They're untangling! It must be another one of your magic powers!"

Soon, the brambles had untangled

completely and there was a clear pathway to the squirrel. Lauren edged closer. Hoping it wouldn't turn around and bite her, she gently released its tail from the prickly bramble.

It was free! Lauren wriggled back. The squirrel looked at its tail and suddenly seemed to realize it was no longer trapped. It scampered out into the clearing and up a nearby tree. With a joyful flick of its tail, it vanished into the leaves.

Lauren smiled. "It's going to be OK," she said, putting her arm over Twilight's neck and giving him a hug. "I'm glad we could help."

"Me, too," he agreed.

Taking hold of his mane, Lauren swung
herself onto his back. A glow of happiness
spread inside her. Using Twilight's magic
to help animals or people always felt great!
"Come on. Let's fly some more," she said.

"OK," Twilight replied eagerly.

Holding tight to his mane, Lauren
laughed out loud as he plunged into
the sky.

When Lauren woke up the next morning,
she didn't feel tired at all. She jumped out
of bed and pulled on her clothes. She had
the whole weekend in front of her!

"We're going to have fun this morning,
Twilight," she said happily as she brushed

him after breakfast. "When I'm finished grooming you, we'll go to Mel's house and go riding, and then you can go out in the field with Shadow and Sandy while Mel, Jess, and I do our project."

Twilight snorted.

Lauren heard the sound of Max giggling and looked around. He was dragging a large plank of wood across the concrete area next to Twilight's field. Buddy was frolicking around him, getting in his way.

"Get off, Buddy!" Max said, sounding half-exasperated, half-amused.

Lauren went over to the fence. "What are you doing?"

"Setting up some stuff to make

skateboard ramps. Dad's going to come out in a minute and help me."

"Do you want a hand?"

"Yes, please," Max replied.

Lauren climbed the fence and took one end of the heavy plank. Buddy bounded around in excitement, almost tripping Max.

"Buddy! Stop it!" Max exclaimed.

As he lowered his end of the plank, Buddy banged into his legs. Max lost his grip and dropped the plank on his toe. "Ow!" he cried, hopping up and down.

"Are you OK?" Lauren asked.

"Yeah," her brother replied, rubbing his toe. "Dumb dog!" Buddy whined.

"Buddy's not dumb. He was just trying to play," Lauren protested. She looked at

the confused dog. Buddy wasn't normally
quite so wild. "Have you taken him out
for a walk this morning?"

Max looked down, his cheeks turning pink.

"Max?" Lauren questioned. "You
have taken him for his morning walk,
haven't you?"

"Well . . . no," Max admitted. "I've been designing my new skateboard course since I got up. I haven't had time."

"Max, you can't not walk him!" Lauren exclaimed. "No wonder he's acting so crazy."

"I'll do it later," Max said. He went over to Buddy and grabbed his collar. "Come on, Buddy. You can stay in the house. You're just getting in the way."

"Max . . ." Lauren started to protest.

Just then, their dad came walking up to the gate. "Hi, you two!" Seeing Max pulling Buddy by the collar, he frowned. "What are you doing, Max?"

"Putting Buddy inside," Max answered.

"I guess it'll be easier if he's out of our way," Mr. Foster agreed.

Lauren wondered what she should do. Her dad didn't know Buddy hadn't been walked that day. She didn't want to get her brother into trouble, but he was being really unfair. "Max," she hissed. "Buddy needs to have some exercise!"

Max ignored her and marched on.

"What time are you going to Mel's?" her dad called.

"Um . . . I said I'd be there at nine-thirty," Lauren answered, turning to him.

"You'd better get a move on, then," Mr. Foster pointed out.

Lauren headed across the field toward Twilight. "Oh, Twilight, I don't know what to do," she said when she reached him. "I feel really sorry for Buddy, but I don't want to tell Dad because then he'll be mad at Max."

Twilight nudged at his empty feed bucket with his nose. Then he looked at her with his intelligent dark eyes.

Lauren frowned. "Your bucket? Food?" Suddenly, she worked out what he was trying to say. "You mean I could give Buddy some food? That's a great idea! I could stuff some treats in his rubber toy. That should keep him busy. Thanks, Twilight!"

Twilight tossed his head and Lauren gave him a hug, thinking for the thousandth time how great it was to have a unicorn!

* A Touch of Magic *

CHAPTER

Four

Getting the toy ready for Buddy made Lauren late but she didn't care. She felt much happier knowing that Buddy had something to do while he waited for Max.

Mel and Jessica were saddled up, waiting for her.

"Let's go for a ride in the fields," Mel suggested.

The three girls rode down the farm trail. The sun was shining and the ponies snorted eagerly, pulling at their bits. Patting Twilight's smooth neck and looking at Sandy's and Shadow's pricked ears, Lauren felt a wave of happiness. It was wonderful to be out riding with her friends on such a beautiful spring morning. She couldn't think of anything she would rather be doing — apart from flying, of course!

When they got back from their ride, Lauren, Mel, and Jessica untacked the ponies and turned them out.

"Where's Samantha this weekend?" Lauren asked Jessica.

Samantha was Jessica's stepsister and
they shared Sandy.

"She's visiting her dad," Jessica replied.
"She's going to stay with him until tomorrow night." She took off her hat and
shook her short blond hair. "Should we
get started on the project?"

Lauren nodded and they went to find
Mel, who was in the tack room.

"We can do the project over there," Mel said, pointing to a large wooden chest where the horses' brushes and clean saddlecloths were kept. It was covered in sheets of paper, horse books, and felt-tip pens. "I thought we could do some big posters."

"That's a great idea," Lauren agreed. "You could do some cartoons on them."

They settled down to work. Lauren and Jessica made a poster showing the different colors and breeds of horses, and Mel made another with funny cartoon drawings showing how *not* to look after a pony. In one cartoon there was a rider facing the wrong way; in another, someone was trying to groom a pony with a vacuum cleaner.

"These posters look really good," Jessica said admiringly after they'd been working an hour.

Mel nodded. "I'm still worried about doing our talk last, though. You know what the boys in the class are like when they get bored. They'll probably start acting really dumb."

They exchanged worried looks.

"It'll be fine," Lauren said, trying to be optimistic. "The other groups might not have cartoons."

Looking slightly reassured, Mel and Jessica went back to work on the posters.

Lauren felt nervous. She'd better be right!

★ ★ ★

At lunchtime, Lauren rode home. As
she took Twilight to his stable, she
heard someone call her name. Her dad
and Max were waving to her from
the new skateboard area. It had been
transformed. Where once there had
been just concrete, there was now a
low rail, a small ramp, a steeper ramp,
and a couple of milk crates arranged
into a jump.

"What do you think, Lauren?" Mr.
Foster called.

"It looks really good," Lauren replied.

"We just finished," her dad said. "Max
was about to try it out."

"Watch me, Lauren! Watch!" Max
insisted.

Putting his helmet on, he set off around
the course. He was slightly wobbly on his
skateboard, but he managed to get up both
ramps and back down, only falling off
once. He even tried a jump where the
board stayed glued to his feet while he was
in the air.

"That's an Ollie," he called proudly. "I'm going to practice and practice until I'm as good as Steven and Leo. I want to learn how to do a kick flip next. That's when the board flips as you jump." His eyes shone.

Lauren smiled. "That's great, Max."

She rode Twilight over to the fence
and dismounted. "I just don't get
skateboarding at all," she said quietly to
her pony as she ran the stirrups up the
leathers. "I mean, so someone can
jump and turn the board under their
feet — what's the big deal?" She thought
for a moment. "I guess that's how some
people must feel about riding and horses,"
she decided.

Untying Twilight, she turned him out.
Then she began to rinse Twilight's feed
buckets. It would be good to get them
cleaned before she went inside.

"Come on, Max. Let's go get some
lunch!" Mr. Foster called.

Max and their dad walked over to her.

"What did you think of my skateboarding, Lauren?" Max asked eagerly.

"It looked great," Lauren told him, emptying the water out of one of the buckets. It formed a muddy puddle on the ground.

Max stroked his skateboard lovingly, brushing away some tiny specks of dust. "I can't wait to tell Steven and Leo about my new ramps!"

Just then, there was a loud woof and Buddy came charging down the path.

"Mom must have let Buddy out," Mr. Foster said. "Easy, boy!" he called to the excited dog.

But Buddy took no notice. He charged straight up to Max, his enormous paws splashing into the muddy puddle.

"Buddy! No!" Max said with a gasp.

Lauren leaped back just in time. Water went all over Max and his skateboard.

"Oh, Buddy!" Max yelled, looking at his muddy skateboard. "Look what you did!"

CHAPTER

Five

Buddy sat down and thumped the tip of his tail uncertainly on the ground. "I'm going to have to wash my skateboard now!" Max said angrily.

"It was an accident, Max," said Mr. Foster. "Buddy didn't mean any harm. It's OK, Buddy." Buddy jumped up and looked hopefully at Mr. Foster. "What is it, boy? You look like you want something."

Buddy trotted forward and pushed his head against him.

"Max?" Mr. Foster said suddenly. "You *have* walked Buddy today, haven't you?"

"Um . . ." Max caught Lauren's eye. "Well . . . not exactly," he admitted. "You see, I was busy and —"

"Max!" Mr. Foster exclaimed. "Poor Buddy. Go take him for a walk right now."

"But it's lunchtime!" Max protested.

"Well, you'll have to wait," their father said firmly. "Animals come first. And don't look at me like that," he added as Max made a face. "I'm very disappointed in you."

"I'm sorry," Max muttered. "I guess I *should* have walked Buddy."

Mr. Foster nodded. "Yes, you should.
You should take a page out of your sister's
book. She's always spending time with
Twilight, grooming him, feeding him,
noticing when there's something wrong."
He smiled at her, but Lauren felt a little
awkward. Twilight was easy to look
after — after all, he could talk to her. And
yes, she did spend a lot of time with him,

but some of the time was when he was a unicorn. Her dad didn't know that!

"Go on, off you go," Mr. Foster said to Max. "Lauren, are you coming in for lunch?"

Lauren hesitated. She felt sorry for Max. "It's OK, Dad. I'll walk Buddy with Max."

Max looked at her in surprise.

"OK." Mr. Foster shrugged. "I'll see you both in the house when you get back." He walked off.

"Dad's really annoying," Max grumbled.

"He only said what he said because he cares about Buddy," she said as they set off down the path.

"Buddy's fine," Max insisted.

"You *have* been neglecting him a little," Lauren ventured.

"I haven't!" Max said defensively. Buddy bounded over. "See, he's happy."

"Yes — now," Lauren replied. "But he looked really miserable this morning. You have to start giving him more attention, Max."

"I do give him attention!" Max protested. "You're just making a big deal about nothing. Buddy's fine!"

"Yeah, right," Lauren said. "You forgot his supper yesterday, you didn't walk him today —"

"If you're going to nag me, I'll walk on my own," Max said sullenly.

Lauren sighed. "OK, let's not argue."
Buddy trotted up to her and she stroked
his head. "Come on, let's play hide-and-
seek with Buddy."

Max nodded, cheering up. "I'll
hide first."

Hide-and-seek was one of Buddy's
favorite games. Max and Lauren took turns
hiding for Buddy to find them. Then they

had him jump over some low obstacles they made out of branches and fallen logs.

"This is fun!" Max exclaimed as he sprang over a small log with Buddy beside him.

"It is," Lauren said, grinning.

After a while, they headed back to the farmhouse for lunch. Max was in a much better mood.

"Thanks for walking with me, Lauren," he said. "Sometimes it can be kind of lonely taking Buddy for walks."

Lauren frowned. She hadn't thought about it before but it *must* be lonely for Max. She had Mel and Jessica to go riding with and even if they weren't there, Twilight could talk to her if she turned him into a unicorn. Max didn't have *any-one* to talk to when he was walking Buddy.

"It's too bad you don't have any friends with dogs nearby," she said. "What about Steven and Leo? Do they like dogs?"

Max shrugged. "I don't know. We only ever talk about skateboarding." The farm-house came into view. "Come on!" he exclaimed. "I'll race you. I'm starving!"

For the rest of the afternoon, Lauren kept thinking about what Max had said. It was no wonder he was spending so much time with Steven and Leo; they were the only boys who lived within walking distance of the farm. Lauren hadn't thought about

Max being lonely before and she wished there was a way to help him.

"Can you think of anything we could do, Twilight?" she asked that evening when she turned him into a unicorn.

Twilight looked thoughtful. "Maybe Max could come out on his bike with Buddy when we ride in the woods?"

Lauren considered it. "Yes, and we could go for picnics together. If I did more with Max, he might look after Buddy better." She felt more cheerful. "I'll ask him to come for a walk tomorrow."

"That's a good idea." Twilight nuzzled her. "Come on, let's go flying now!"

CHAPTER
Six

The following morning, Lauren found Max in the kitchen with Buddy. "Would you like to do something with Buddy and Twilight this morning?" she suggested. "We could go into the woods. You could ride your bicycle and I could ride Twilight."

"OK," Max said eagerly.

"We can go after breakfast," Lauren

said, putting a piece of bread in the
toaster.

"I've had my breakfast," Max said. Just
then, the phone rang. Max picked it up.
"Granger's Farm," he answered. A smile
spread across his face. "Hi, Steven. Yeah,
I'd love to come over. You'll never guess
what — Dad and I built some ramps here!"
There was a pause. "OK. I'll go ask my
mom if I can come now."

Max put the phone down. "That was
Steven," he explained. "He invited me
over, so I won't be able to go to the
woods with you."

The kitchen door opened and Mrs.
Foster came in. "Mom! Can I go to Steven
and Leo's?" Max asked.

"Sure," Mrs. Foster said. "But you have to walk Buddy first."

"Oh . . ." Max started to complain but he seemed to notice their mom's eyebrows raise. "OK." He sighed. "I'll do it now."

"Make sure it's a good long walk," Mrs. Foster added as he pulled on his sneakers. "Dad said you didn't walk him yesterday

until lunchtime. That's not fair, Max. If you're going to have a dog you have to look after him properly. You know how strongly Dad and I feel about your pets being your responsibility."

"I know." Max shrugged. "Come on, Buddy."

He opened the door and Buddy bounded out.

"What are you going to do this morning, honey?" Mrs. Foster asked Lauren as she put the tea kettle on.

"I think I'll call Mel and see if we can finish our project," Lauren replied.

"Well, I'll be in my study if you need me," Mrs. Foster said. She made herself a cup of coffee and went back to work.

Lauren had just finished her toast when Max came back.

"Did you forget something?" she asked in surprise.

"No, I finished walking Buddy," Max replied.

"But that wasn't a long enough walk," Lauren said, looking at Buddy, who was standing hopefully by the door. "You were only out five minutes."

"Yeah, but Steven said to come over right away," Max said. "I'll walk Buddy again later. He'll be fine." He grabbed his skateboard. "See you, Lauren!"

"Max!" Lauren started to protest, but the door had already banged shut.

Buddy scratched at the door and

whined. Lauren walked over and gave him a pet. She could take him out for a walk herself but Mom or Dad might see her, and then Max would get into trouble for not walking Buddy himself. And now she'd arranged to go to Mel's house to finish their project. She couldn't leave Mel and Jessica to do it all on their own.

"I'll take you out at lunchtime if Max hasn't walked you," she promised Buddy. She got out a dog bone from the cupboard. Buddy chewed it listlessly.

Lauren felt awful as she let herself out of the house. *Poor Buddy,* she thought as she hurried down the path to Twilight's field.

* * *

When Lauren got to Mel's house, the three girls decided to go for a ride in the woods before continuing with their project.

"We could go to the creek and skip stones," Mel suggested.

"Cool," Jessica agreed.

Lauren nodded, but she couldn't get Buddy out of her thoughts. Was he still waiting by the door?

Mel and Jessica tacked up and they rode into the woods. After a while, Mel looked at Lauren. "You're very quiet. Is everything OK?"

"I'm worried about Buddy," Lauren admitted. "Max isn't taking good care of him." She told the others what was going on. "If Mom and Dad find out he hasn't been walked today, they'll be really mad, and Buddy's so unhappy."

"Can't you say something to Max?" Jessica asked.

"I've tried, but he just says Buddy's happy and I'm worrying about nothing . . ."

She broke off with a gasp as something big, black, and furry burst out of the

bushes beside them. The three ponies shied in alarm.

"Buddy!" Lauren exclaimed as the Bernese mountain dog skidded to a stop.

"Steady, Sandy!"

Hearing Jessica's alarmed cry, Lauren swung around. Sandy, who was young and easily startled, was racing backward with her eyes rolling. Jessica had lost her stirrups.

"Hang on, Jess!" Mel cried out as Sandy half-reared up in fear. Jessica grabbed for a handful of mane, but she lost her grip and slipped off Sandy's back, landing on the ground with an uncomfortable thud.

"Whoa, Sandy!" Lauren cried as the palomino pony cantered toward her. She tried to grab Sandy's reins but her fingers closed around thin air.

In a thunder of hooves, Sandy galloped off down a side trail into the trees.

"Sandy!" all three girls cried.

Mel looked around and, seeing Jessica still on the ground, leaped off Shadow. "Jess? Are you OK?"

"I'm fine," Jessica said, scrambling to her feet. "But we've got to catch Sandy!"

Buddy trotted toward Shadow. Mel grabbed his collar.

"Twilight's the fastest. I'll go after Sandy!" Lauren said.

"OK," Mel said.

Tears were streaking down Jessica's face. "Please catch her, Lauren! *Please!*"

CHAPTER

Seven

Twilight needed no encouragement. Plunging forward, he galloped in the same direction as Sandy.

Lauren bent low over his neck, her heart pounding. Where was Sandy? The pony could go deeper and deeper into the woods and get lost completely. Or maybe she'd find her way onto a road. Or to the old quarry with its steep dangerous sides . . .

"Oh, Twilight, we've got to catch her!" Lauren cried.

Twilight weaved in and out of the trees. The forest grew thicker with every stride. He started to slow down, every so often jumping over a twisted tree root. The trees were too close together for him to gallop safely.

An image of Sandy lying injured filled Lauren's mind. "Twilight, please! Go as fast as you can!" she begged.

To her surprise, Twilight stopped. Lauren lurched forward onto his neck. "What are you doing?" Twilight stamped his front hoof and whinnied and, suddenly, Lauren knew what he was trying to say. "It'll be quicker if we fly?"

Twilight nodded.

Lauren glanced around. It was broad daylight, and even though they were deep in the heart of the woods, it would be really risky to turn Twilight into a unicorn now. Someone might see him. But they had to stop Sandy.

"OK," she whispered. She quickly said the words of the Turning Spell.

In a second, Twilight was a unicorn.

"Sandy went this way," he said. "I can see her hoofprints and there are some cream-colored hairs on that branch over there. She's heading toward the quarry, but if I fly fast we might be able to cut her off!"

"Be as quick as you can," Lauren begged. "Sandy could really hurt herself!"

Twilight plunged into the air and they flew through the treetops, just skimming the branches.

"There!" Lauren shouted, catching a glimpse of gold through the trees. "I think I see her!"

"I'll fly down," Twilight said.

Lauren saw the deep jagged pit of the quarry as they circled above it, and then Twilight swooped to the ground. As he landed on a clear patch of rock, Lauren heard the sound of Sandy's hooves.

"She's coming!"

Sandy burst out of the trees. Her eyes were wide with fear. One of her stirrup leathers had come off and her reins were trailing dangerously around her legs. She was heading straight for the edge of the quarry!

Twilight stepped onto the trail and lifted his head. A ray of sunshine filtered through the leaves, lighting up his silver horn and making it sparkle.

With a snort, Sandy slowed down.

Twilight blew out softly and stepped toward her. Bending his head, he let his horn touch her neck. Lauren guessed that he was using his magic power to calm her fear. As Lauren watched, the terror gradually faded from Sandy's eyes. Her breathing slowed and she stopped trembling.

Slipping off Twilight's back, Lauren walked up to the palomino pony. "It's

OK, girl," she murmured, reaching out for the pony's reins.

Sandy whinnied. Twilight nickered back.

"What's she saying?" Lauren asked.

"She says she was really frightened by Buddy jumping out," Twilight explained. "She didn't realize it was him."

"Oh, Sandy," Lauren said, smoothing the palomino's white forelock. "You silly thing. Come on, let's get you back to Mel and Jessica."

Twilight looked around. "I guess you should turn me back into a pony first, Lauren. We're near the main trail here and someone might see me."

Lauren said the words of the Undoing Spell and remounted. Then, holding on to Sandy's reins, she led her back through the trees.

Mel and Jessica were waiting where Lauren had left them. Jessica was crying. Mel had one arm around her, with her other hand firmly holding on to Buddy's collar.

"Sandy!" Jessica said with relief when Lauren appeared with the ponies. She raced over. "Is she OK?"

"Her reins are broken but she's fine," Lauren replied, handing Sandy's reins to Jessica and dismounting.

Jessica flung her arms around her pony's neck and hugged her hard. "Oh, Sandy, I was so worried."

Sandy nuzzled her.

"She was just startled by Buddy," Lauren explained. She caught herself quickly. "I mean, I *think* that's why she galloped off." She looked at Buddy.

"Buddy, what were you doing in the woods?"

Buddy panted, his tongue hanging out of his mouth. He looked like he was smiling, but Lauren saw him lick his lips and wag just the tip of his tail, two signs that he was feeling confused. "Come on." She sighed, stroking his ears. "I'd better take you home." She looked at Mel. "I'll take Buddy back and then come over."

"OK," Mel agreed. "We'll take Shadow and Sandy home."

Lauren brought Twilight's reins over his head and, holding on to Buddy's collar with the other hand, she started to trudge home through the woods.

"I guess you were probably trying to

find Max," she said to the dog. "Well, I hope I can get you back in the house without Mom or Dad seeing that you've been out on your own."

But as she turned on to the trail that led to Twilight's field, her heart sank. Her mom and dad were both near Twilight's stable, calling Buddy's name.

Pulling away from Lauren's hand, Buddy bounded down the trail to meet them.

"Hey, where did you find Buddy?" Mr. Foster asked in surprise.

"Er, he was in the woods," Lauren replied. She decided not to mention the fact that Buddy had scared Sandy and made Jessica fall off.

"He escaped from the kitchen," Mrs.

Foster said. "I think he must have pressed the handle down when he was pawing at the door. I saw him go past the study window, toward Twilight's stable. I called him but he didn't stop." She shook her head. "It's very strange. He normally never runs off. Max *did* walk him this morning, didn't he, Lauren?"

"Um . . ." Lauren really didn't want to

get Max into trouble. "Yes. He . . . he *did* take him out."

Mr. Foster seemed to hear the hesitation in her voice. He looked at her shrewdly. "For a real walk?"

Lauren felt her cheeks go red. "Not exactly."

Mrs. Foster looked angry. "But I *told* Max he wasn't to go to Steven and Leo's until he'd walked Buddy." She shook her head. "I'm very annoyed with him. In fact, I'm going over there right now to bring him home."

"Oh, Mom, please don't . . ." Lauren protested. She knew how embarrassed Max would be to have their mom turn up to drag him home.

"No, Lauren. Max has gone too far this time. He's been neglecting Buddy ever since he started skateboarding."

Lauren bit her lip as her mom and dad set off up the path.

"Oh, Twilight," she whispered. "Max is in real trouble now."

Lauren waited with Twilight until she heard her mom's car coming back down the driveway. Hurrying up the path, she saw Max getting out of the car. "It's not fair," he was shouting. "Why did I have to come home?"

"You *know* why, Max," Mrs. Foster said, getting out, too. "I asked you to walk

Buddy before you went to your friends'
and you didn't."

"I did!"

"You didn't take him out for long
enough. Lauren told us."

Max glared at his sister. "Thanks,
Lauren!"

"Don't take it out on her," Mrs. Foster
scolded. "You should have taken Buddy
out for a real walk. He escaped into the
woods this morning. Anything could have
happened."

"But nothing did," Max protested.

Lauren was very glad she hadn't men-
tioned Sandy's fall. Max and Buddy were
in enough trouble already.

"That's not the point," Mrs. Foster said. "Buddy's your responsibility, and if you can't look after him, Dad and I are not going to let you keep him. We'll find him another home."

"No!" Max gasped.

"Mom!" Lauren exclaimed.

"I mean it, Max," Mrs. Foster said
firmly. "I will *not* see an animal neglected."

"But Buddy's not neglected." Max
stamped his foot. "You're not being fair!"

"Go to your bedroom please, Max.
We'll talk about this when you've
calmed down."

Max ran into the house, slamming the door behind him.

Lauren stared at her mom. "Mom, you wouldn't really give Buddy away, would you?"

Mrs. Foster ran a hand through her hair. "I'm sorry, Lauren. I know you love Buddy. I do, too. But I can't stand by and see Max make him unhappy." She sighed. "I just hope Max gets the message."

Lauren looked up at her younger brother's bedroom window. *Oh, Max,* she thought. *Please start looking after Buddy better. Please!*

CHAPTER

Eight

Lauren didn't sleep well that night.
She couldn't stop worrying about
Max. He had looked after Buddy for the
rest of the day, feeding him and brushing
him, but he had done it sulkily and
Lauren had noticed their mom frowning
as she watched him. *If only Buddy could
talk to him like Twilight can talk to me,*
Lauren thought as she turned over

restlessly in bed. *Then he'd be able to tell Max how he feels.*

The next day, Lauren found herself yawning as some of her classmates presented their projects. Even though she loved ponies, it was hard to pay attention when Jade's group began the second talk of the day on how to look after a pony.

"This is a dandy brush," Jade said, pointing to a picture that was too small for the rest of the class to see. "And this is a body brush." She pointed to another picture. "And this is a currycomb."

"We've heard all this!" Adam Neil called out. "David's group did horses this morning!"

"Tell us something different," said Adam's friend Simon. "This is boring!"

"Settle down, please, boys," Mrs. Bradshaw, their teacher, said. "Just listen."

Mel shot Lauren a worried look. Lauren guessed what she was thinking. If people were bored now, how were they going to feel listening to a third presentation about horses? *We've got to make our talk more interesting,* she thought desperately. *But how?*

On the way home from school, Lauren, Max, and Mrs. Foster stopped at Mrs. Fontana's shop so Mrs. Foster could pick up a book she had ordered.

The doorbell tinkled as they walked in

and Walter, Mrs. Fontana's terrier, trotted over to meet them.

"Hello," Mrs. Fontana said, appearing from the back of the old-fashioned shop. She was wearing a yellow shawl and her gray hair was held back in a bun. "You must be here to pick up your book."

"Yes, please," Mrs. Foster replied.

"Do you have any books on skate-boarding, Mrs. Fontana?" Max asked.

Mrs. Fontana smiled. "There are some in the children's section. Take a look if you want, Max."

"Thanks," Max said. He hurried to the back of the shop.

Mrs. Fontana turned to Lauren. "Lauren, would you mind giving me a hand in the storeroom? I put your mom's book on a high shelf, but my arthritis is acting up today and I would be very grateful if you would help me get it down."

While her mom browsed, Lauren followed Mrs. Fontana to the back of the shop and through a curtain of glass beads that glittered and sparkled. Lauren had never been in the storeroom before. The shelves that lined the narrow walls were packed with books, and there was a small desk in one corner.

"How's Twilight?" Mrs. Fontana asked.

"Great," Lauren replied. "We discovered that he can untangle thorns with his magic."

"Ah, yes, that's the power he has to make order out of chaos," Mrs. Fontana

nodded. "Very useful." She grabbed a low
stepladder. "Your mother's book is on the
second shelf. If you could just reach it for
me, that would be a great help."

"Sure." Lauren climbed up and took
the book down.

Mrs. Fontana smiled. "Thank you,
my dear."

As she passed her the book, Lauren
noticed how stiff Mrs. Fontana's fingers
were. "Couldn't Twilight use his magic to
cure your arthritis, Mrs. Fontana?" she asked,
thinking about how Twilight had once
used his magic to heal cuts on her hands.

Mrs. Fontana shook her head. "My
arthritis comes from old age. I'm afraid
even unicorn magic can't cure that."

"Oh," Lauren said.

Mrs. Fontana's blue eyes studied Lauren. "You look worried about something, my dear."

"Two somethings, actually," Lauren admitted. "A school project I'm doing, and Max." She told Mrs. Fontana everything that had been happening. "It's awful," she finished. "Mom's serious about finding Buddy another home if Max doesn't start looking after him better." She looked hopefully at Mrs. Fontana. "There isn't anything Twilight and I can do, is there?"

"I'm afraid that this is one of those problems — just like my arthritis — that can't be solved by unicorn magic," Mrs. Fontana said. "It sounds to me like Max has become so caught up in his new hobby that he's forgotten how much Buddy means to him and how much *he* means to Buddy. But neither you nor Twilight can make him realize that."

Lauren sighed. "The thing is, I *know* Max loves Buddy deep down. He just doesn't seem to understand what he's feeling." She sighed. "If only there was some way Buddy could speak to Max, like Twilight can talk to me."

Mrs. Fontana smiled. "Oh, Lauren. All animals can talk. People just need to listen."

"What do you mean?" Lauren asked.

Mrs. Fontana's eyes crinkled up at the corners. "You don't need me to explain. If you think about it, my dear, I'm sure you'll work it out on your own. And it might just help you with your problems, too."

Lauren didn't have time to ask Mrs. Fontana what she meant before they went back through the curtain into the shop.

Lauren's mom and Max were standing

by the counter. "We'd better get going," said Mrs. Foster.

Mrs. Fontana rang up the purchase on the cash register. "See you again soon," she called as they left.

"Bye, Mrs. Fontana," Lauren replied. She was still thinking about what Mrs. Fontana had said in the storeroom. *"All animals can talk. People just need to listen."* What did she mean? Animals couldn't talk. Well, apart from Twilight, and that was only because he was a unicorn.

"I just don't get it," she said as she groomed Twilight a little while later. "Animals can't talk. What did Mrs. Fontana mean?"

Twilight stamped his hoof. Just then, Lauren noticed a patch of mud on his stomach just where his girth would go. She started to brush at it quickly. Twilight threw his head up and swished his tail.

"What's the matter?" Lauren asked. "Was I being too rough? Sorry." She began to brush more carefully, this time using smooth, gentle strokes.

Twilight relaxed and Lauren smiled. Sometimes she didn't need him to be a unicorn to understand what he was saying.

Her eyes widened.

"Of course! That's what Mrs. Fontana means!"

Twilight looked around at her.

"She *wasn't* saying that animals can speak to people like you talk to me when you're a unicorn. She meant that animals can communicate with people in other ways. Like when you put your ears back, I know that means you're unhappy, and when you stamp your hoof, you're impatient."

Twilight tossed his head.

A thought struck Lauren. "And it's not just ponies, is it? Other animals can talk to people, too. Maybe that's what Mrs. Fontana meant about Max. If he can watch Buddy closely and understand what he's saying, he'll find it easier to look after him —" She broke off.

She'd just had the perfect idea for the school project!

CHAPTER

Nine

"What do you think?" Lauren asked, looking at Mel and Jessica a little while later. "How about we do our project on how ponies talk to us?"

Mel and Jessica were staring at her as if they thought she'd gone crazy.

"But Lauren," Jessica said, "ponies don't talk."

"They do!" Lauren insisted. "Sure, they

don't open their mouths and speak words, but they tell us what they're thinking by the way they move their ears and heads and tails. I think we should do our project on how ponies" — she searched for the right word — "how they *communicate*."

Mel and Jessica still didn't look convinced.

"Watch." Lauren led Twilight over to where Shadow was tied up. Shadow pricked his ears and the two ponies touched noses. "They're saying hello. Breathing out through their nostrils is their way of greeting each other — or us." She walked up to Shadow and he obligingly lifted his head and blew on her face. "See, he's saying hello to me!"

"I guess so. I hadn't really thought about it as talking," Mel said.

"I know, but that's what it is," Lauren said. "And I think the rest of our class would be really interested if we did our project on this."

Jessica nodded. "We could still use our posters and things, but if we did this as well, it would be lots better than just doing another talk on how to take care of a horse."

"Yes," Mel agreed. "I know — how about we make a *video* of our ponies and show it to the class?"

"That's a great idea!" Lauren exclaimed. "We could tape the ponies doing different things and explain to the class what they're saying with their body language. We could even take some regular photos and get the class to guess what moods the ponies have in each picture."

The three girls looked at one another excitedly.

"No one would be bored if we did that," Mel said. "I'll go ask my mom if I can borrow our video camera."

Luckily, Mrs. Cassidy agreed and the three girls set about filming Shadow, Sandy, and Twilight. Twilight was wonderful. He swished his tail when Lauren groomed his stomach, and put his ears forward and whickered when Lauren walked up to him. He tossed his head when Lauren did

his girth up too tight, and stamped his hoof when she rattled his feed bucket.

"It's like he understands what we want!" Mel exclaimed.

Lauren hid a grin. There were some *definite* advantages to Twilight being a unicorn!

The girls worked until the sun was setting and it was time for Lauren to ride home.

"I'll ask my mom to bring me back as soon as I've fed Twilight and turned him out in the field," she promised.

"OK. We'll put Sandy and Shadow away and start looking at the video," said Mel.

When Lauren reached Twilight's stable, she saw Max practicing on his skateboard. He was jumping in the air and trying to turn the board under his feet.

Remembering that she'd been meaning to talk to him about Buddy, Lauren untacked Twilight and went to the gate. "Max," she called. "Can I talk to you for a minute?"

"Not now," Max replied. "Steven and Leo are coming over tomorrow and I want

to be able to do this kick flip perfectly."
He turned his skateboard around and
tried again.

Lauren hesitated. *I'll talk to him later,* she
decided, and she went back to Twilight.

But when Lauren finally got back from
Mel's house that night, it was eight-thirty
and Max had already gone to bed.

I guess I'll just have to wait till the morning,
she decided. Kicking off her boots, she
headed upstairs to take a shower.

The next morning, Max was already up
and practicing on his skateboard when
Lauren went outside to give Twilight his
breakfast.

"Max!" Lauren called, waving to him. "Come over here."

"I can't," Max replied. "I'm practicing."

"I want to talk to you about Buddy," Lauren said, going over to him. "I don't think you understand what he's thinking a lot of the time, and that makes it hard for you to look after him."

Max looked confused.

"Think about when he wags his tail," Lauren persisted. "Sometimes it means he's happy, but sometimes it means he's confused or worried. It depends on *how* he wags his tail. There are other things as well, like how he pricks his ears and if he's panting or not. They're all ways he tries to talk to you."

Max didn't look convinced. "Yeah, right." He got on his skateboard again.

"Max, this is important!" Lauren protested. "I really can help you to understand Buddy better —"

"Some other time," Max said, and he began to skate away from her.

Feeling frustrated, Lauren watched him go before heading back to the tack room. She needed to feed Twilight and get ready for school. Butterflies fluttered in her stomach at the thought of presenting their project that afternoon.

She mixed Twilight's feed and took it to the paddock. "I hope the other kids like all the stuff we've done about horses," she told him.

He lifted his head and snorted reassuringly. Bits of grain fell onto Lauren's jeans, but she didn't care. She knew he was just trying to tell her that everything would be fine. She hugged him.

"Thanks, Twilight," she said, feeling better. "I'll come see you as soon as I get home and tell you all about it."

She gave him a kiss, then climbed over the gate and hurried back to the house.

CHAPTER

Ten

Lauren, Jessica, and Mel were the very last group to present their project. The previous talk had been on stick insects, and even Mrs. Bradshaw had looked as if she was having trouble staying awake.

"Well, it's time for the last presentation," she announced, sounding relieved. "Lauren, Mel, Jessica, would you come up, please?"

"Not another talk on horses!" Adam complained.

"Oh, no," Simon groaned.

"Well, it's not a talk about how to look after a horse," said Lauren as she walked up to the front with Mel and Jessica following. "It's about how horses communicate."

"Yes," Jessica backed her up. "And how people can tell what horses are thinking."

The class looked more interested.

"OK," Mrs. Bradshaw said. "Now, you told me you'd like to use the VCR. It's all set up, so when you're ready, you can start."

"Cool! We get to watch TV," Adam said, looking more cheerful.

Lauren exchanged looks with Mel and Jessica. They had agreed that she would start. Taking a deep breath, she smiled at the class. "Our project is called 'Animals can talk, if only people would listen.' We're going to show you how ponies communicate and how easy it is to understand what they're trying to say." She glanced at Mel. "Mel, can you start the video, please?"

To Lauren, Jessica, and Mel's relief, their talk was a great success. The whole class listened while they showed them the video and talked about what the ponies were doing. Then Jessica handed out the photos they'd printed and they

split the class into groups to guess the

ponies' moods.

There was a picture of Twilight with

his ears back, one of Sandy pawing the

ground, one of Shadow with his ears

pricked in excitement, and a picture of

Twilight nuzzling Lauren affectionately.

Even Adam and Simon joined in and

called out suggestions. Mel finished by

holding up her posters. Everyone loved Mel's cartoons, and Mrs. Bradshaw said she would put them up on the classroom wall.

"That was a fascinating project!" she said when the girls were finished. "You should be very proud of yourselves — and your ponies. They posed beautifully for the photos and it was clear exactly what they were saying."

"It was cool!" Adam called out.

Someone started to clap and the whole class joined in. Lauren, Mel, and Jessica blushed and exchanged pleased smiles.

Just then, the bell rang. With the sound of the applause still ringing in their ears, the three girls headed for the coatroom.

"I can't believe it went so well!" Mel exclaimed.

"You were great, Lauren," Jessica said. "You explained everything perfectly."

Lauren grinned. She felt proud but also very relieved. It was over and it had been a success. She couldn't wait to get home and tell Twilight all about it!

When she went into the school yard, she was surprised to see Steven and Leo standing with Max; then she remembered that they were coming home with him to play.

All the way back to the farm, the boys talked about skateboarding.

As soon as Mrs. Foster pulled up outside

the farmhouse, Max jumped out of the car. "The ramps are this way!"

"Max!" Mrs. Foster said. "Maybe Steven and Leo want to get a drink first."

"We're fine, thanks," Steven said politely. "Aren't we, Leo?"

Leo nodded. "We'd really love to see the skateboard stuff, Mrs. Foster."

"OK," Mrs. Foster said, smiling. "Off you go!"

The boys grabbed their skateboards and helmets and hurried off. Mrs. Foster turned to Lauren. "Steven and Leo are nice, aren't they?"

Lauren nodded. "Yeah, though a bit skateboard obsessed. I thought Max was bad enough!"

Mrs. Foster headed for the house. "Are you coming in?"

"I'll just go see Twilight first," Lauren replied. She ran down the path toward Twilight's paddock. He was waiting at the gate.

"Hi, boy," Lauren said, patting him. "The project was great! Everyone loved the video."

On the other side of the field, the boys

were already on their skateboards. "Watch this!" Max called. He jumped in the air and flipped his board.

"Way to go!" Steven said.

Max looked very proud. "I can do a kick flip after coming down a ramp, too."

"Are you sure, Max?" Leo said. "That's really difficult."

"Yeah," Steven said doubtfully. "You haven't been skating that long."

"Watch!" Max insisted. He skated up to the highest ramp.

Just then, there was the sound of thundering paws. Lauren turned to see Buddy charging down the path from the house. He galloped straight toward Max just as he started coming down the ramp, his face frowning in concentration.

Max looked up in alarm as Buddy woofed, and his skateboard wobbled. Max's arms flailed wildly, but it was too late and the skateboard flipped over.

"Oh, no!" Lauren cried as Max crashed to the ground. She ran to the fence. "Are you OK, Max?"

Buddy jumped on top of Max, his tail wagging like crazy.

"I'm fine. Get off, Buddy!" Max shouted. "You stupid dumb dog!" He clambered to his feet. His cheeks were bright red with embarrassment.

"Are you sure you're all right?" Steven

said, hurrying over to him. "That was a bad fall."

"It was a really difficult move to try," Leo agreed. "Especially since you haven't been skateboarding that long."

Lauren saw tears of humiliation in her brother's eyes. "I'd have been fine if it hadn't been for Buddy. I only fell off because of him." He turned to Buddy. "I hate you! You always wreck everything. Well, I hope Mom and Dad do give you away after all!"

With that, he turned and ran into the house.

There was an awkward silence. Buddy sat down and whined.

"Oh, Buddy," Lauren said. Buddy came

trotting over to her and thrust his nose into her hand.

Steven looked at his younger brother. "You shouldn't have said that, Leo. You made it sound like Max was just a little kid. He might have managed the jump if he hadn't been distracted by the dog."

Leo looked awkward. "I just meant it was a difficult jump for a beginner." He looked at Lauren. "I didn't mean to upset Max."

Lauren sighed. "Don't worry. I think he was just embarrassed about falling off."

Steven walked over to her. "Is this your dog?"

"No, he's Max's," Lauren replied. "Hasn't Max ever told you about him?"

"No," Steven replied. "But then we

always just talk about skateboarding. He stroked Buddy's head. "Hi there, fella."

Buddy's tail thumped on the ground.

Leo started petting him, too. Buddy jumped up and pushed against Leo's legs, almost knocking him over. Leo laughed.

"What should we do about Max?" Steven said.

"I don't think there's anything you *can* do," Lauren said. "It's best to give him a chance to calm down. I'll go see him in a minute."

"I guess we should go home, then," Steven said to Leo. "It doesn't seem right to practice on Max's ramps without him."

"Will your mom or dad be home?" Lauren asked.

"Mom will," Steven replied. "Tell Max to come find us if he wants. He can bring his skateboard over."

The two boys gave Buddy one last pat and set off. Buddy made a move to follow them but Lauren grabbed his collar. "No, you don't, Buddy."

Buddy whimpered and tried to pull away after the boys.

Lauren sighed. She knew she should go see how Max was. She walked up to the house with Buddy. When she got to the backdoor she stopped. "Maybe you should wait here, Buddy. I'm not sure Max will want to see you right now." She could still hear Max's words ringing in her ears. *I hate you . . . I hope Mom and Dad do give you away.* She was sure Max had only said those things because he'd been feeling humiliated. But what sort of mood would he be in now?

As she reached the top of the stairs, she heard the sound of Max crying.

"Max?" Lauren said, pushing his bedroom door open. "Max? Are you OK?"

Her brother was sprawled on his bed. "Go away!"

"Max, don't cry. There's nothing to be upset about."

"Yes there is. Steven and Leo think I'm just a dorky little kid."

"No they don't," Lauren protested, going and sitting on his bed.

"They do. I fell off my skateboard."

"So? I'm sure everyone falls off," Lauren told him. "It's like riding. The important thing is that you get back up and try again."

"I guess," Max muttered. He sniffed. "I just wish Leo and Steven hadn't been there. I feel so stupid."

"Don't worry," Lauren said. "Leo and Steven won't care about you falling off. They're your friends. It's like Jessica and

Mel. They don't laugh at me if I make mistakes on Twilight. They make me feel better."

There was silence as Max thought about what she'd said. "Really?"

"Really," Lauren told him.

The tears started to dry on Max's face. "Where are Leo and Steven now?"

"They went home. I think they felt a little awkward," Lauren replied. "But they told me to tell you to go see them. They said to bring your skateboard."

"So they *do* still want to be friends with me?" Max asked.

Lauren nodded.

Max looked relieved. "I'll go over right now," he said, getting up and heading for the door.

"Max," Lauren said. He stopped and looked at her. "You weren't very nice to Buddy just now," she told him. "He didn't mean any harm. He was just excited to see you. If you'd gone to see him when you got home, he wouldn't have come racing out like that."

Max hesitated. "I guess." He looked rather ashamed. "I didn't really mean those things I said, you know."

"I know, but it upset Buddy," Lauren told him. "He couldn't understand why you were shouting at him just for saying hello."

Max bit his lip. "All right. I'll tell him everything's OK. Where is he?"

"Outside," Lauren replied.

They went down to the kitchen. "Buddy! Here, boy!" Max called, opening the door.

But Buddy didn't appear.

"Buddy! Where are you?" Max called again.

Lauren grabbed Buddy's metal bowl and banged it. It was a sound that usually made Buddy come running. But not this time.

"Where is he?" Max frowned.

"I don't know," said Lauren, starting to feel worried. "I left him here."

"It's not like Buddy to wander off," Max said. "Maybe it's because I shouted at him." His eyes widened and his face went pale. "Oh, Lauren!" he exclaimed. "Do you think he ran away?"

CHAPTER

Eleven

Lauren stared at her brother. "Ran away?"

"I said I hated him!" Max burst out. "I said I didn't want him anymore. He might have thought I meant it!" He ran outside. "Buddy!" he called. "Come back. I didn't mean any of those things!"

But still no Buddy.

Tears started to well in Max's eyes. "Buddy! *Buddy!*"

Lauren felt her heart beat faster. "We'd better tell Mom," she said. "Come on!"

Mrs. Foster was very concerned to hear that Buddy had disappeared. "He didn't even come back when you banged his food bowl?" she asked Lauren.

Lauren shook her head.

"I said I hated him, Mom. He ran away and it's all my fault!" Max said, tears running down his face.

"Calm down, Max," Mrs. Foster said. "Buddy wouldn't run away just because of something you said."

"I bet he would!" Max said, his words coming out in a sob. "He thinks I don't want him, but I do!"

"Do you want me to go look in the woods with Twilight?" Lauren offered.

"Thanks, honey," Mrs. Foster said. "I'll tell your dad and we'll search here on the farm."

Lauren gave Max a quick hug. "We'll find Buddy. Don't worry!"

She raced down the path. If she could just get Twilight into the woods and turn him into a unicorn, she could use his magic to find out where Buddy was. When Twilight touched his horn to rose quartz, he could see anyone he wanted *and* see where they were.

Twilight whinnied when he saw her.

"Buddy's disappeared," Lauren told him. "You didn't see him go, did you?"

Twilight shook his head.

"We've got to find him," Lauren said. "Let's go to the clearing in the woods so you can use your magic to look for him!"

She put Twilight's bridle on but didn't bother with his saddle. "Come on!" she said, leading him out of the field and swinging herself onto his back.

As Twilight cantered into the woods, Lauren clung to his mane. Riding him bareback was much easier when he was in his magical shape and he had unicorn magic to keep her on!

Twilight leaped over a tree root in
the path.

"Steady, boy!" Lauren said with a gasp.

Just then, she heard the faint sound of
barking. "That sounds like Buddy!" she
exclaimed.

She looked and looked, but the trees
were so thick she couldn't see anything.

She hesitated. Should they follow the noise or keep going to the clearing?

Woof! Woof! The bark was faint but it *definitely* sounded like Buddy. Twilight pulled toward the trees.

Lauren made up her mind. "OK, Twilight. If you think it's Buddy, let's go that way."

Twilight started to weave in and out of the trees as the path faded away. Ducking under branches, Lauren felt her heart pounding. Where was Buddy?

She remembered how he'd spooked Sandy and made her run off. What if he caused another accident? What if he was in an accident himself? An icy shiver ran down her spine.

The woofing was coming from the
edge of the woods where there were
houses — and a road.

"Hurry, Twilight!" Lauren urged, feeling sick with worry.

Suddenly, Twilight stopped. There was
a low fence ahead marking out the bound-
ary between the woods and the yards
behind the houses. But a deep thicket of
blackberry bushes blocked the way to
the fence.

"Oh, no!" Lauren exclaimed in dismay.

She heard another bark. It seemed to
come from just on the other side of the
fence. *Oh, Buddy*, Lauren thought desperately, *please don't be in trouble!*

"We'll have to go back," she told

Twilight. "We can't
get through this
way." But to her sur-
prise, Twilight didn't
move when she pulled
the rein. "Twilight!"
she exclaimed.

Twilight tossed his
head and stamped
his hoof.

Lauren frowned. She had a feeling he
was trying to tell her something. But what?

Twilight pushed at the bushes with
his nose.

In a flash, Lauren realized what he'd
been trying to say. *His magic powers!* He
could use them to untangle the blackberry

branches! "You want me to turn you into a unicorn?"

Twilight nodded.

Lauren looked around. She was desperate to get to Buddy but it was very risky to turn Twilight into a unicorn in broad daylight. Still, the trees were really thick between her and the houses. She decided to take the risk.

Scrambling off Twilight's back, she said the magic words.

In a flash, Twilight turned into a unicorn. "I can use my magic to try to clear a path by untangling the brambles," he explained.

"Do you think it will work?" Lauren asked. These bushes were much thicker than the place where the squirrel had been trapped.

Twilight looked determined, and his horn glowed even brighter. "I'll try!"

He lowered his horn to the branches and, sure enough, the briars started to unravel! Twilight took a step forward, touching his horn to the next tangle of branches. Little by little, a narrow pathway appeared.

"You're doing it, Twilight!" Lauren cried in delight.

As the last brambles unwound themselves, Lauren's impatience got the better of her and she forced her way through. Ignoring the scratches on her arms, she ran to the fence and peered over.

"Twilight! It *is* Buddy!"

The fence bordered a long yard with a large house at the far end. Near the house was a hard tennis court with various pieces of skateboarding equipment on it — a ramp, a quarter pipe, and several jumps. Two boys were rolling around on skateboards, and playing with them and woofing excitedly was Buddy!

Lauren felt a wave of relief rush through her. Buddy was safe. He wasn't on the road and he wasn't in trouble.

"It's Leo and Steven," Twilight said, joining Lauren at the fence. "This must be their house."

"I wonder what Buddy's doing here," Lauren said.

"Maybe he got bored waiting outside

your house and decided to follow Leo and Steven home," Twilight suggested.

Lauren nodded. She felt trembly with relief. "I'm so glad he's not in trouble. Should we go into the yard and get him? The fence is low. You could easily jump it."

"OK," Twilight agreed. "But you'd better change me back first."

Lauren grinned. "Yes. I think I'd better." Steven and Leo seemed to like dogs, but she had a feeling they'd be pretty surprised to see a real live unicorn in their yard!

She said the Undoing Spell and cantered Twilight up to the fence. He leaped over it easily.

The boys looked around. Seeing

Lauren and Twilight, Buddy barked joy-
fully and ran over. "Oh, Buddy," Lauren
said, getting off Twilight and hugging him.
"We were so worried about you!"

"How did you get here?" Steven asked
in surprise.

"I jumped over the fence," Lauren said.
"I was looking for Buddy in the woods
and I heard him barking."

"But what about the blackberry
bushes?" Steven asked. "They're really
thick on the other side of the fence."

"Oh, I found a way through," Lauren
said quickly. "How long has Buddy
been here?"

"He got here about ten minutes ago,"
said Leo. "He came trotting into the yard
as if he wanted to come and play with us."

"Max will be so happy to know he's
safe," Lauren said. "I should go tell him
Buddy's here."

"Or I could call Max and let him know
right away," Steven suggested.

"Yes, please!" Lauren replied.

Steven set off toward the house. Leo
stroked Twilight. "He's great."

"Thanks." Lauren smiled. "Do you like animals?"

"I love them," Leo said. "Steven does, too. We used to have a dog, a golden retriever named Jake, but he died last year. It's been really weird without him." He brightened slightly. "But Mom and Dad say we can get another dog now that we've moved to the country.

Maybe it could be friends with
Buddy."

"Yeah!" Lauren exclaimed. "That
would be great!"

Buddy wagged his tail and woofed.

Five minutes later, there was the sound of a
car in the driveway and Max came tearing
into the yard. "Buddy!"

Buddy charged over to him. He stopped too late and almost sent Max flying, but Max didn't care. He flung his arms around the dog. "Buddy, I'm so glad you're all right. I promise I'll never be mean to you again."

Buddy licked his face. "Yuck!" Max exclaimed, but then he laughed and hugged Buddy even harder.

Mrs. Foster came around the corner. "Hello, Steven. Hello, Leo. I'm very glad you found Buddy."

"Well, actually he found us," Steven said.

"Whichever way it was, I'm just glad he's safe," Mrs. Foster replied. She looked at Lauren. "You did well to track him down."

Lauren smiled. "Twilight helped."

Twilight snorted proudly.

"You know, sometimes I'm sure Twilight can understand every word you say," Mrs. Foster commented.

Lauren stroked Twilight to hide her grin.

"Come on, Max. Should we take Buddy home?" said Mrs. Foster.

Lauren saw Leo's and Steven's faces fall. "Couldn't Max and Buddy stay here for a while?" she said.

"Yes, please!" Steven exclaimed.

"But I haven't got my skateboard," Max said.

"That's fine. We can play with Buddy instead," said Steven.

Buddy woofed.

"We love dogs!" Steven told Max. "We're going to get a puppy soon."

"We'll be able to take our new dog and Buddy for walks together," Leo added.

Max looked delighted. "Cool!"

"Come on," urged Steven. "I bet Buddy will love running up and down the ramps and doing the jumps."

"I'll come back in an hour," Mrs. Foster told Max.

"OK. See you later, Mom!" Max called, and he ran off after Leo and Steven, with Buddy bounding around them.

"See you at home, Lauren," said Mrs. Foster.

Lauren nodded and got back on

Twilight. The boys were charging around the skateboard course with Buddy beside them. Lauren watched for a moment.

"I'm glad it all worked out OK," she murmured to Twilight.

He whickered in agreement.

"Come on," she said softly. "Let's go home."

As they started up the yard, Max ran over. "Lauren? Thanks for finding Buddy. I'm never going to be mean to him ever again."

"Good." Lauren smiled.

Max hesitated. "And . . . um . . . you know what you were saying this morning, about how I can learn to tell what Buddy's thinking by looking at his tail and ears?

Well, will you help me learn that stuff?"
He looked hopefully at Lauren. "I'd really
like to know what Buddy's saying."

"Of course I'll help you," Lauren
told him.

"Thanks. I want to make him happy,"
Max vowed. "When I thought he'd run
away, it was awful."

Lauren glanced across to where Buddy
was playing with Leo and Steven. "He sure
looks happy now."

Max grinned. "He does, doesn't he? I'll
see you later, Lauren!" And with that, he
ran back to join the others.

Lauren rode Twilight toward the fence.
He cleared it easily again.

As the trees closed around them, Lauren slipped off his back and said the Turning Spell. With a purple flash, Twilight turned into a unicorn.

"We did it," he said in delight. "We found Buddy!"

"Yes, and it looks like Max isn't going

to find it so lonely looking after him from now on." Lauren leaned her head against Twilight's neck and breathed in his warm, sweet smell. "Thanks for helping, Twilight."

"That's OK." Twilight nuzzled her.

"I love you, Twilight," Lauren whispered, hugging him hard.

They stood there for a moment, and then Lauren said the Undoing Spell. Twilight turned back into a pony and, climbing onto his back, Lauren rode him through the trees.

As the dusk gathered around them and Twilight's hooves thudded on the forest floor, Lauren felt as if they were lost in their own little private world. She looked at Twilight's pricked ears. She knew she'd love him even if he couldn't talk, even if he was just a regular pony.

All ponies are special, she thought. *And they can all talk to us if we just listen.*

She stroked Twilight's neck and smiled. All ponies *were* special, but unicorns were very special indeed.

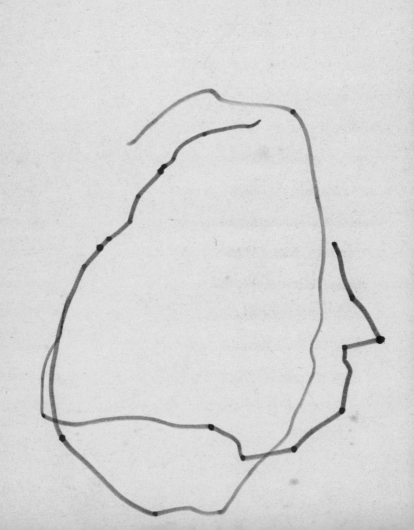